an's love ✦ *As flies to wanton boys are we to th'gods; they kill us for their* d-

nettle danger we pluck   this flower safety ✦ Love looks not with the eyes, but with the

Darkness is a gentleman ✦ The time is out of joint ✦ *The end crowns all, and that old common*

eople in't! ✦ 'Tis the eye of childhood that fears a painted devil ✦ Why then, the world's mine oyster ✦

✦ Something is rotten in the state of Denmark ✦ *Though this be madness, yet there is method in't*

do not, 'tis no great matter there ✦ The primrose way to the everlasting bonfire ✦ Nothing will come

vasty deep. *Why, so can I, or so can any man; but will they come*   when you do call for

to be kind ✦ Necessity's sharp pinch ✦ The lady   protests too much,

with less art ✦ *There are more things in heaven*   and earth, Horatio,

That which we call a rose by any other word would smell as sweet ✦ Delays have dangerous ends ✦

My kingdom for a horse! ✦ It is the bright day that brings forth the adder ✦ *I love long life*

ely the shadow of a dream   ✦ To gild refinèd gold, to paint the lily . . . is wasteful and

Truth will come to light;   murder cannot be hid long ✦ *Beware the ides of*

ery acquaints a man with   strange bedfellows ✦ A peace is of the nature of a

echanicals ✦ A man   can die but once. We owe God a death ✦ *Naught's*

des like a leather jerkin ✦ *Give thy thoughts no tongue, nor any unproportioned thought his act* ✦

are the best men ✦ Give every man thine ear but few thy voice ✦ The labour we delight in physics

What's done is done ✦ It was Greek to me ✦ *There is no virtue like necessity* ✦ They say a made a

but being in, bear't that th'opposèd may beware of thee ✦ Things sweet to taste prove in digestion

To be wise and love exceeds man's might ✦ *How hard it is for women to keep counsel!* ✦ Sweet

weet prince,   and flights of angels sing thee to thy rest ✦ There's small

is to look into happiness through another man's

e can   say, "This is the worst" ✦ Patch grief with

ld" ✦ Adversity's sweet milk, philosophy ✦ *Time travels in divers paces with divers persons*

SOMETHING RICH AND STRANGE

A Treasury of Shakespeare's Verse

KINGFISHER
Larousse Kingfisher Chambers Inc.
95 Madison Avenue
New York, New York 10016

First American edition 1995
2 4 6 8 10 9 7 5 3 1

LIBRARY OF CONGRESS CATALOGING-IN-PUBLICATION DATA
Something rich and strange: a treasury of Shakespeare's verse/
[compiled by Gina Pollinger: illustrated by Emma Chichester Clark.]
—1st American ed.
p.   cm
Includes bibliographical reference and indexes
Summary: Thematically arranged excerpts from Shakespeare's plays and sonnets.
1. Shakespeare, William, 1564-1616—Quotations. 2. Quotations, English.
[1. Shakespeare, William, 1564-1616—Quotations. 2. Quotations.]
1. Pollinger, Gina. II. Chichester Clark, Emma. ill. III. Title.
PR2771. P58 1995   95-3008
822.3'3—dc20 CIP AC

ISBN 1-85697-597-5

The extracts from Shakespeare's verse contained in this selection
are reprinted by permission of Oxford University Press
from *The Complete Works of William Shakespeare*
edited by Stanley Wells and Gary Taylor (O.U.P. 1988).
Copyright © Oxford University Press 1988.
The sources of the quotations also refer to
this edition.

The quotation from *Poetry for You* by
C. Day-Lewis is reprinted by permission
of Peters, Fraser & Dunlop Group Ltd.

Designed by Caroline Johnson
Edited by Caroline Walsh
Printed in Slovenia

SOMETHING RICH AND STRANGE

A Treasury of Shakespeare's Verse

SELECTED BY
GINA POLLINGER

ILLUSTRATED BY
EMMA CHICHESTER CLARK

Kingfisher
NEW YORK

Poetry has the same effect on words as wet sand on pennies. In what seems almost a miraculous way, it brightens up words that looked dull and ordinary.

"Don't let the playground bullies tell you that poetry is soft... a good poem is just about as hard as a diamond... think of the things you know that have the longest lives—yew trees, tortoises, marble temples, ancient castles. Well, a good poem can live on for centuries longer than a tortoise or a yew tree."

C. Day-Lewis *Poetry for You* (Basil Blackwell, 1944)

✦ CONTENTS ✦

✦ INTRODUCTION ✦

Something Rich and Strange is directed, purely and simply, at those who read for pleasure. Those encountering Shakespeare's sixteenth-century language for the first time can take comfort from the words of the eighteenth-century critic, Dr. Johnson, who observed that Shakespeare's creations "act and speak as the reader thinks he himself should have spoken or acted on the same occasion ... the dialogue is level with life." Shakespeare, as actor and playwright, spent his entire working life burrowing under the skin of character, male and female, young and old, heroic and hapless, rustic and royal. He slips easily into all our shoes—even in the twentieth century!

The imagery that links Shakespeare's powerful imagination to our own may be startling in color, form, and meaning, but it draws upon objects that are universally familiar. These range from the homespun—such as milk, meat, drink, salad, slipper—to the world of nature—stars, moon, weed, lily, snail, and so on. A perfect marriage of sound to sense ensures and enhances the effect:

> Then was I as a tree
> Whose boughs did bend with fruit; but in one night
> A storm or robbery, call it what you will,
> Shook down my mellow hangings, nay, my leaves,
> And left me bare to weather.

> *Cymbeline, act III, scene iii*

Such underlying simplicity demonstrates that Shakespeare's poetry and poetic drama were indeed written for all to enjoy, irrespective of social class and education.

This anthology is an orchestrated succession of relatively short clusters and sequences—all in the "rattling tongue of saucy and audacious eloquence"—linked in theme, extract to extract, section to section. The touchstone is immediacy, the keynote, almost always, passion: Shakespeare's verse was meant to be spoken, not read, and you will find the sense more obvious and the current of feeling twice as stirring, if you read aloud. Brief quotations act as headings at the top of each page—some merry, some somber, some magic, some moody. My aim in including them was to smooth the flow and reinforce atmosphere, manner, and direction. It may sound like a contradiction in terms but, from the first, I planned this anthology as a single composition, an overture that would pave the way and make access to Shakespeare that much easier.

In one sense, any anthology is likely to be unsatisfactory: something important must be missing! Since *Something Rich and Strange* is an anthology of Shakespeare's poetry—not Shakespeare's poetic drama—character and plot are the inevitable casualties. Yet, isolating the poetry does yield positive benefits. It concentrates the mind on the flexibility and range of Shakespeare's chosen medium, blank verse. It also demonstrates that Shakespeare's poetry enjoys a life of its own, regardless of dramatic context. When a besieged and bereaved Macbeth surrenders to despair, the details of his personal tragedy become, for the moment, curiously unimportant:

> Tomorrow, and tomorrow, and tomorrow
> Creeps in this petty pace from day to day,
> To the last syllable of recorded time,
> And all our yesterdays have lighted fools
> The way to dusty death. Out, out, brief candle.
> Life's but a walking shadow, a poor player
> That struts and frets his hour upon the stage,
> And then is heard no more. It is a tale
> Told by an idiot, full of sound and fury,
> Signifying nothing.
>
> *Macbeth, act V, scene v*

The poetry speaks for itself and, in this particular case, for anyone who has—even for one moment—given up hope.

There are, of course, dark elements in this anthology, as there are in life itself, but good humor, sweet reason, beauty, and reconciliation predominate. You have only to look at the endpapers, at the words of wit and wisdom strung across them, to feel your spirits rise. For Shakespeare took neither himself nor his art too seriously. Here he is poking fun at poetry and playing to the crowd:

> I had rather be a kitten and cry "mew",
> Than one of these same metre ballad-mongers.
> I had rather hear a brazen canstick turned,
> Or a dry wheel grate on the axle-tree,
> And that would set my teeth nothing on edge,
> Nothing so much as mincing poetry.
> 'Tis like the forced gait of a shuffling nag.
>
> *Henry IV, Part I, act III, scene i*

Mincing poetry? Yes, Shakespeare was a master of self-mockery, too!

Something Rich and Strange is an attempt to convey in miniature a faithful impression of the richness, gusto, intelligence, and scope of Shakespeare's poetry. I hope the selection will prove more than a browser's delight: that some of you will be encouraged to look beyond it to even more spectacular discoveries—this time in the live theater. For there you will hear this poetry—and much more, on themes now familiar—happily restored to character, plot, and stage: Shakespeare in action, Shakespeare in the round, Shakespeare in all his glory.

GINA POLLINGER

For my mother
Whose delight in all things beautiful
continues to inspire me.
G. P.

POWER TO CHARM

Come unto these yellow sands,
And then take hands.

The Tempest, act I, scene ii

Be not afeard. The isle is full of noises,
Sounds, and sweet airs, that give delight and hurt not.
Sometimes a thousand twangling instruments
Will hum about mine ears, and sometime voices
That if I then had waked after long sleep
Will make me sleep again; and then in dreaming
The clouds methought would open and show riches
Ready to drop upon me, that when I waked
I cried to dream again.

The Tempest, act III, scene ii

Under the greenwood tree
   Who loves to lie with me,
   And turn his merry note
   Unto the sweet bird's throat,
Come hither, come hither, come hither.
   Here shall he see
   No enemy
But winter and rough weather.

Who doth ambition shun,
   And loves to live i'th' sun,
   Seeking the food he eats
   And pleased with what he gets,
Come hither, come hither, come hither:
   Here shall he see
   No enemy
But winter and rough weather.

As You Like It, act II, scene v

And this our life, exempt from public haunt,
Finds tongues in trees, books in the running brooks,
Sermons in stones, and good in everything.

As You Like It, act II, scene i

Daffodils,
That come before the swallow dares, and take
The winds of March with beauty…
…pale primroses,
…bold oxlips,
…lilies of all kinds.
The Winter's Tale, act IV, scene iv

Hot lavender, mints, savory, marjoram,
The marigold, that goes to bed wi'th' sun,
And with him rises, weeping.
The Winter's Tale, act IV, scene iv

And winking Mary-buds begin
to ope their golden eyes;
With everything that pretty is,
my lady sweet, arise,
Arise, arise!
Cymbeline, act II, scene iii

Merrily, merrily
shall I live now
Under the blossom that
hangs on the bough.
The Tempest, act V, scene i

I know a bank where the wild thyme blows,
Where oxlips and the nodding violet grows,
Quite overcanopied with luscious woodbine,
With sweet musk-roses, and with eglantine.
There sleeps Titania sometime of the night,
Lulled in these flowers with dances and delight;
And there the snake throws her enamelled skin,
Weed wide enough to wrap a fairy in.

A Midsummer Night's Dream, act II, scene i

Where the bee sucks, there suck I:
In a cowslip's bell I lie;
There I couch when owls do cry.
On the bat's back I do fly.

The Tempest, act V, scene i

Over hill, over dale,
   Thorough bush, thorough brier,
Over park, over pale,
   Thorough flood, thorough fire:
I do wander everywhere
Swifter than the moonës sphere,
And I serve the Fairy Queen
To dew her orbs upon the green.
The cowslips tall her pensioners be.
In their gold coats spots you see;
Those be rubies, fairy favours;
In those freckles live their savours.
I must go seek some dewdrops here,
And hang a pearl in every cowslip's ear.

A Midsummer Night's Dream, act II, scene i

You spotted snakes with double tongue,
   Thorny hedgehogs, be not seen;
Newts and blindworms, do no wrong;
   Come not near our Fairy Queen.

Weaving spiders, come not here;
   Hence, you long-legged spinners, hence;
Beetles black, approach not near;
   Worm nor snail do no offence.

   Philomel with melody,
   Sing in our sweet lullaby;
Lulla, lulla, lullaby; lulla, lulla, lullaby.
     Never harm,
     Nor spell nor charm
   Come our lovely lady nigh.
   So good night, with lullaby.

A Midsummer Night's Dream, act II, scene ii

She bids you on the wanton rushes lay you down
And rest your gentle head upon her lap,
And she will sing the song that pleaseth you
And on your eyelids crown the god of sleep,
Charming your blood with pleasing heaviness.

Henry IV, Part I, act III, scene i

Peaseblossom, Cobweb, Mote, and Mustardseed!
Be kind and courteous to this gentleman.
Hop in his walks, and gambol in his eyes.
Feed him with apricots and dewberries,
With purple grapes, green figs, and mulberries;
The honeybags steal from the humble-bees,
And for night tapers crop their waxen thighs
And light them at the fiery glow-worms' eyes
To have my love to bed, and to arise;
And pluck the wings from painted butterflies
To fan the moonbeams from his sleeping eyes.
Nod to him, elves, and do him courtesies.

A Midsummer Night's Dream, act III, scene i

Through the house give glimmering light.
  By the dead and drowsy fire
Every elf and fairy sprite
  Hop as light as bird from brier,
And this ditty after me
Sing, and dance it trippingly.

First rehearse your song by rote,
To each word a warbling note.
Hand in hand with fairy grace
Will we sing and bless this place.

A Midsummer Night's Dream, act V, scene ii

Light thickens, and the crow
Makes wing to th' rooky wood.
Good things of day begin to droop and drowse,
Whiles night's black agents to their preys do rouse.

Macbeth, act III, scene ii

'Tis now the very witching time of night,
When churchyards yawn, and hell itself
  breathes out
Contagion to this world.

Hamlet, act III, scene ii

The time has been
That, when the brains were out, the man would die,
And there an end. But now they rise again
With twenty mortal murders on their crowns,
And push us from our stools.

Macbeth, act III, scene iv

In the most high and palmy state of Rome,
A little ere the mightiest Julius fell,
The graves stood tenantless, and the sheeted dead
Did squeak and gibber in the Roman streets.

Hamlet, act I, scene i

Now o'er the one half-world
Nature seems dead, and wicked dreams abuse
The curtained sleep. Witchcraft celebrates
Pale Hecate's offerings, and withered murder,
Alarumed by his sentinel the wolf,
Whose howl's his watch, thus with his stealthy pace,
With Tarquin's ravishing strides, towards his design
Moves like a ghost.

Macbeth, act II, scene i

What are these
So withered, and so wild in their attire,
That look not like th'inhabitants o'th'earth,
And yet are on't?

Macbeth, act I, scene iii

FIRST WITCH

When shall we three meet again?
In thunder, lightning, or in rain?

SECOND WITCH

When the hurly-burly's done,
When the battle's lost and won.

THIRD WITCH

That will be ere the set of sun.

FIRST WITCH

Where the place?

SECOND WITCH

Upon the heath.

THIRD WITCH

There to meet with Macbeth.

FIRST WITCH

I come, Grimalkin.

SECOND WITCH

Paddock calls.

THIRD WITCH

Anon.

ALL

Fair is foul, and foul is fair,
Hover through the fog and filthy air.

Macbeth, act I, scene i

FIRST WITCH

Round about the cauldron go,
In the poisoned entrails throw.
Toad that under cold stone
Days and nights has thirty-one
Sweltered venom sleeping got,
Boil thou first i'th' charmèd pot.

ALL

Double, double, toil and trouble,
Fire burn, and cauldron bubble.

SECOND WITCH

Fillet of a fenny snake,
In the cauldron boil and bake.
Eye of newt and toe of frog,
Wool of bat and tongue of dog,
Adder's fork and blind-worm's sting,
Lizard's leg and owlet's wing,
For a charm of powerful trouble,
Like a hell-broth boil and bubble.

ALL

Double, double, toil and trouble,
Fire burn, and cauldron bubble...

SECOND WITCH

By the pricking of my thumbs,
Something wicked this way comes.
Open, locks, whoever knocks.

MACBETH

How now, you secret, black, and midnight hags,
What is't you do?

ALL

A deed without a name.

Macbeth, act IV, scene i

The night has been unruly. Where we lay
Our chimneys were blown down, and, as they say,
Lamentings heard i'th' air, strange screams of death,
And prophesying with accents terrible
Of dire combustion and confused events
New-hatched to th' woeful time. The obscure bird
Clamoured the livelong night. Some say the earth
Was feverous and did shake.

Macbeth, act II, scene iii

I have heard
The cock, that is the trumpet to the morn,
Doth with his lofty and shrill-sounding throat
Awake the god of day, and at his warning,
Whether in sea or fire, in earth or air,
Th'extravagant and erring spirit hies
To his confine.

Hamlet, act I, scene i

Good morrow, masters, put your torches out.
  The wolves have preyed, and look, the gentle day
Before the wheels of Phoebus round about
  Dapples the drowsy east with spots of grey.

Much Ado About Nothing, act V, scene iii

Lo, here the gentle lark, weary of rest,
From his moist cabinet mounts up on high
And wakes the morning, from whose silver breast
The sun ariseth in his majesty,
  Who doth the world so gloriously behold
  That cedar tops and hills seem burnished gold.

Venus and Adonis, lines 853–858

Night's candles are burnt out, and jocund day
Stands tiptoe on the misty mountain tops.
Romeo and Juliet, act III, scene v

Even till the eastern gate, all fiery red,
Opening on Neptune with fair blessèd beams
Turns into yellow gold his salt green streams…
A Midsummer Night's Dream, act III, scene ii

Kissing with golden face the meadows green,
Gilding pale streams with heavenly alchemy.
Sonnet 33

YOUTH, I DO ADORE THEE!

Crabbèd age and youth
Cannot live together:
Youth is full of pleasance,
Age is full of care;
Youth like summer morn,
Age like winter weather;
Youth like summer brave,
Age like winter bare.
Youth is full of sport,
Age's breath is short.
Youth is nimble, Age is lame,
Youth is hot and bold,
Age is weak and cold.
Youth is wild, and Age is tame.
   Age, I do abhor thee;
   Youth, I do adore thee.
     O my love, my love is young.
   Age, I do defy thee.
     O sweet shepherd, hie thee,
For methinks thou stay'st too long.

The Passionate Pilgrim, Part 12

Behold, my lords,
Although the print be little, the whole matter
And copy of the father: eye, nose, lip,
The trick of's frown, his forehead, nay, the valley,
The pretty dimples of his chin and cheek, his smiles,
The very mould and frame of hand, nail, finger.

The Winter's Tale, act II, scene iii

But thou art fair, and at thy birth, dear boy,
Nature and Fortune joined to make thee great.
Of Nature's gifts thou mayst with lilies boast,
And with the half-blown rose.

King John, act II, scene ii

Thou art thy mother's glass, and she in thee
Calls back the lovely April of her prime.

Sonnet 3

VALERIA
How does your little son?

VIRGILIA
I thank your ladyship; well, good madam.

VOLUMNIA
He had rather see the swords and hear a drum
than look upon his schoolmaster.

VALERIA
O' my word, the father's son!

Coriolanus, act I, scene iii

We were, fair Queen,
Two lads that thought there was no more behind
But such a day tomorrow as today,
And to be boy eternal.

The Winter's Tale, act I, scene ii

We were as twinned lambs that did frisk i'th' sun,
And bleat the one at th'other. What we changed
Was innocence for innocence. We knew not
The doctrine of ill-doing, no, nor dreamed
That any did. Had we pursued that life,
And our weak spirits ne'er been higher reared
With stronger blood, we should have answered heaven
Boldly, "Not guilty", the imposition cleared
Hereditary ours.

The Winter's Tale, act I, scene ii

I was too young that time to value her,
But now I know her. If she be a traitor,
Why, so am I. We still have slept together,
Rose at an instant, learned, played, eat together,
And wheresoe'er we went, like Juno's swans,
Still we went coupled and inseparable.

As You Like It, act I, scene iii

Is all the counsel that we two have shared—
The sisters' vows, the hours that we have spent
When we have chid the hasty-footed time
For parting us—O, is all quite forgot?
All schooldays' friendship, childhood innocence?
We, Hermia, like two artificial gods
Have with our needles created both one flower,
Both on one sampler, sitting on one cushion,
Both warbling of one song, both in one key,
As if our hands, our sides, voices, and minds
Had been incorporate. So we grew together,
Like to a double cherry: seeming parted,
But yet an union in partition,
Two lovely berries moulded on one stem.

A Midsummer Night's Dream, act III, scene ii

Think not I love him, though I ask for him.
'Tis but a peevish boy. Yet he talks well.
But what care I for words? Yet words do well
When he that speaks them pleases those that hear.
It is a pretty youth—not very pretty—
But sure he's proud; and yet his pride becomes him.
He'll make a proper man. The best thing in him
Is his complexion; and faster than his tongue
Did make offence, his eye did heal it up.
He is not very tall; yet for his years he's tall.
His leg is but so-so; and yet 'tis well.
There was a pretty redness in his lip,
A little riper and more lusty red
Than that mixed in his cheek. 'Twas just the difference
Betwixt the constant red and mingled damask.

As You Like It, act III, scene v

My salad days,
When I was green in judgement.

Antony and Cleopatra, act I, scene v

Some say thy fault is youth, some wantonness.

Sonnet 96

The tongues of mocking wenches are as keen
  As is the razor's edge invisible,
Cutting a smaller hair than may be seen,
  Above the sense of sense; so sensible
Seemeth their conference. Their conceits have wings
Fleeter than arrows, bullets, wind, thought, swifter things.

Love's Labour's Lost, act V, scene ii

SILVIUS

O Corin, that thou knew'st how I do love her!

CORIN

I partly guess; for I have loved ere now.

SILVIUS

No, Corin, being old thou canst not guess,
Though in thy youth thou wast as true a lover
As ever sighed upon a midnight pillow.

As You Like It, act II, scene iv

What is love? 'Tis not hereafter,
Present mirth hath present laughter.
    What's to come is still unsure.
In delay there lies no plenty,
Then come kiss me, sweet and twenty.
    Youth's a stuff will not endure.

Twelfth Night, act II, scene iii

IT WAS A LOVER
AND HIS LASS

It was a lover and his lass,
    With a hey, and a ho, and a hey-nonny-no,
That o'er the green cornfield did pass
    In spring-time, the only pretty ring-time,
When birds do sing, hey ding-a-ding ding,
Sweet lovers love the spring.

As You Like It, act V, scene iii

VALENTINE

Why, how know you that I am in love?

SPEED

Marry, by these special marks: first, you have learned, like Sir Proteus, to wreathe your arms, like a malcontent; to relish a love-song, like a robin redbreast; to walk alone, like one that had the pestilence; to sigh, like a schoolboy that had lost his ABC; to weep, like a young wench that had buried her grandam; to fast, like one that takes diet; to watch, like one that fears robbing; to speak puling, like a beggar at Hallowmas. You were wont, when you laughed, to crow like a cock; when you walked, to walk like one of the lions. When you fasted, it was presently after dinner; when you looked sadly, it was for want of money. And now you are metamorphosed with a mistress, that when I look on you I can hardly think you my master.

The Two Gentlemen of Verona, act II, scene i

He does smile his face into more lines than is in the new map with the augmentation of the Indies. You have not seen such a thing as 'tis. I can hardly forbear hurling things at him.

Twelfth Night, act III, scene ii

Proceed, sweet Cupid, thou hast thumped him
with thy birdbolt under the left pap.

Love's Labour's Lost, act IV, scene iii

I have known when there was no music with
him but the drum and the fife, and now had he
rather hear the tabor and the pipe. I have known
when he would have walked ten mile afoot to see
a good armour, and now will he lie ten nights
awake carving the fashion of a new doublet. He
was wont to speak plain and to the purpose, like
an honest man and a soldier, and now is he turned
orthography. His words are a very fantastical
banquet, just so many strange dishes.

Much Ado About Nothing, act II, scene iii

If thou rememberest not the slightest folly
That ever love did make thee run into,
Thou hast not loved.

As You Like It, act II, scene iv

O coz, coz, coz, my pretty little coz, that thou didst know how many fathom deep I am in love. But it cannot be sounded. My affection hath an unknown bottom, like the Bay of Portugal.

As You Like It, act IV, scene i

He says he loves my daughter.
I think so, too, for never gazed the moon
Upon the water as he'll stand and read,
As 'twere, my daughter's eyes; and to be plain,
I think there is not half a kiss to choose
Who loves another best.

The Winter's Tale, act IV, scene iv

Tell me where is fancy bred,
Or in the heart, or in the head?
How begot, how nourishèd?
   Reply, reply.
It is engendered in the eyes,
With gazing fed.

The Merchant of Venice, act III, scene ii

A lover's eyes will gaze an eagle blind.
A lover's ear will hear the lowest sound.

Love's Labour's Lost, act IV, scene iii

Her lily hand her rosy cheek lies under,
Coz'ning the pillow of a lawful kiss.

The Rape of Lucrece, lines 386–387

O, she doth teach the torches to burn bright!
It seems she hangs upon the cheek of night
As a rich jewel in an Ethiope's ear.

Romeo and Juliet, act I, scene v

O happy fair!
Your eyes are lodestars, and your tongue's sweet air
More tuneable than lark to shepherd's ear
When wheat is green, when hawthorn buds appear.

A Midsummer Night's Dream, act I, scene i

Her voice was ever soft,
Gentle, and low, an excellent thing in woman.

King Lear, act V, scene iii

In love—ay, faith, to the very tip of the nose.

Troilus and Cressida, act III, scene i

JACQUES
What stature is she of?
ORLANDO
Just as high as my heart.

As You Like It, act III, scene ii

I will tell you.
The barge she sat in, like a burnished throne
Burned on the water. The poop was beaten gold;
Purple the sails, and so perfumèd that
The winds were love-sick with them. The oars were silver,
Which to the tune of flutes kept stroke, and made
The water which they beat to follow faster,
As amorous of their strokes. For her own person,
It beggared all description. She did lie
In her pavilion—cloth of gold, of tissue—
O'er-picturing that Venus where we see
The fancy outwork nature. On each side her
Stood pretty dimpled boys, like smiling Cupids,
With divers-coloured fans whose wind did seem
To glow the delicate cheeks which they did cool,
And what they undid did.

Antony and Cleopatra, act II, scene ii

Age cannot wither her, nor custom stale
Her infinite variety. Other women cloy
The appetites they feed, but she makes hungry
Where most she satisfies.

Antony and Cleopatra, act II, scene ii

His legs bestrid the ocean; his reared arm
Crested the world. His voice was propertied
As all the tunèd spheres, and that to friends;
But when he meant to quail and shake the orb,
He was as rattling thunder. For his bounty,
There was no winter in't; an autumn 'twas,
That grew the more by reaping. His delights
Were dolphin-like; they showed his back above
The element they lived in. In his livery
Walked crowns and crownets. Realms and islands were
As plates dropped from his pocket.

Antony and Cleopatra, act V, scene ii

DROMIO OF SYRACUSE

I am an ass, I am a woman's man, and besides myself.

ANTIPHOLUS OF SYRACUSE

What woman's man? And how besides thyself?

DROMIO OF SYRACUSE

Marry, sir, besides myself I am due to a woman: one that
claims me, one that haunts me, one that will have me...
I have but lean luck in the match, and yet is she a
wondrous fat marriage.

ANTIPHOLUS OF SYRACUSE

How dost thou mean, a fat marriage?

DROMIO OF SYRACUSE

Marry, sir, she's the kitchen wench, and all grease; and I
know not what use to put her to but to make a lamp of her,
and run from her by her own light. I warrant her rags and
the tallow in them will burn a Poland winter. If she lives till
doomsday, she'll burn a week longer than the whole world.

The Comedy of Errors, act III, scene ii

LORENZO

The moon shines bright. . . . In such a night
Troilus, methinks, mounted the Trojan walls,
And sighed his soul toward the Grecian tents
Where Cressid lay that night.

JESSICA

                    In such a night
Did Thisbe fearfully o'ertrip the dew
And saw the lion's shadow ere himself,
And ran dismayed away.

LORENZO

                    In such a night
Stood Dido with a willow in her hand
Upon the wild sea banks, and waft her love
To come again to Carthage.

JESSICA

                    In such a night
Medea gatherèd the enchanted herbs
That did renew old Aeson.

LORENZO

                    In such a night
Did Jessica steal from the wealthy Jew,
And with an unthrift love did run from Venice
As far as Belmont.

JESSICA

                    In such a night
Did young Lorenzo swear he loved her well,
Stealing her soul with many vows of faith,
And ne'er a true one.

LORENZO

                    In such a night
Did pretty Jessica, like a little shrew,
Slander her love, and he forgave it her.

The Merchant of Venice, act V, scene i

When you speak, sweet,
I'd have you do it ever; when you sing,
I'd have you buy and sell so, so give alms,
Pray so; and for the ord'ring your affairs,
To sing them too. When you do dance, I wish you
A wave o'th' sea, that you might ever do
Nothing but that, move still, still so,
And own no other function. Each your doing,
So singular in each particular,
Crowns what you are doing in the present deeds,
That all your acts are queens.

The Winter's Tale, act IV, scene iv

ORSINO

How dost thou like this tune?

VIOLA

It gives a very echo to the seat
Where love is throned.

Twelfth Night, act II, scene iv

If music be the food of love, play on,
Give me excess of it that, surfeiting,
The appetite may sicken and so die.
That strain again, it had a dying fall.
O, it came o'er my ear like the sweet sound
That breathes upon a bank of violets,
Stealing and giving odour. Enough, no more,
'Tis not so sweet now as it was before.

Twelfth Night, act I, scene i

Music, moody food of us that trade in love.

Antony and Cleopatra, act II, scene v

But soft, what light through yonder window breaks?
It is the east, and Juliet is the sun.
Arise, fair sun, and kill the envious moon,
Who is already sick and pale with grief
That thou, her maid, art far more fair than she.
Be not her maid, since she is envious.
Her vestal livery is but sick and green,
And none but fools do wear it; cast it off.
It is my lady, O, it is my love.
O that she knew she were!
She speaks, yet she says nothing. What of that?
Her eye discourses; I will answer it.
I am too bold. 'Tis not to me she speaks.
Two of the fairest stars in all the heaven,
Having some business, do entreat her eyes
To twinkle in their spheres till they return.
What if her eyes were there, they in her head?—
The brightness of her cheek would shame those stars
As daylight doth a lamp; her eye in heaven
Would through the airy region stream so bright
That birds would sing and think it were not night.
See how she leans her cheek upon her hand.
O, that I were a glove upon that hand,
That I might touch that cheek!

Romeo and Juliet, act II, scene i

Love's feeling is more soft and sensible
Than are the tender horns of cockled snails.

Love's Labour's Lost, act IV, scene iii

Or as the snail, whose tender horns being hit
Shrinks backward in his shelly cave with pain,
And there, all smothered up, in shade doth sit,
Long after fearing to creep forth again.

Venus and Adonis, lines 1033–1036

That I might sleep out this great gap of time
My Antony is away.
Antony and Cleopatra, act I, scene v

From you have I been absent in the spring
When proud-pied April, dressed in all his trim,
Hath put a spirit of youth in everything,
That heavy Saturn laughed and leapt with him.
Yet nor the lays of birds nor the sweet smell
Of different flowers in odour and in hue
Could make me any summer's story tell,
Or from their proud lap pluck them where they
    grew;
Nor did I wonder at the lily's white,
Nor praise the deep vermilion in the rose.
They were but sweet, but figures of delight
Drawn after you, you pattern of all those;
    Yet seemed it winter still, and, you away,
    As with your shadow I with these did play.
Sonnet 98

Except I be by Silvia in the night
There is no music in the nightingale.
Unless I look on Silvia in the day
There is no day for me to look upon.
The Two Gentlemen of Verona, act III, scene i

Being your slave, what should I do but tend
Upon the hours and times of your desire?
I have no precious time at all to spend,
Nor services to do, till you require;
Nor dare I chide the world-without-end hour
Whilst I, my sovereign, watch the clock for you,
Nor think the bitterness of absence sour
When you have bid your servant once adieu.
Nor dare I question with my jealous thought
Where you may be, or your affairs suppose,
But like a sad slave stay and think of naught
Save, where you are, how happy you make those.
   So true a fool is love that in your will,
   Though you do anything, he thinks no ill.

Sonnet 57

The course of true love never did run smooth.

A Midsummer Night's Dream, act I, scene i

So holy and so perfect is my love,
And I in such a poverty of grace,
That I shall think it a most plenteous crop
To glean the broken ears after the man
That the main harvest reaps. Loose now and then
A scattered smile, and that I'll live upon.

As You Like It, act III, scene v

Let me not to the marriage of true minds
Admit impediments. Love is not love
Which alters when it alteration finds,
Or bends with the remover to remove.
O no, it is an ever fixèd mark,
That looks on tempests, and is never shaken;
It is the star to every wand'ring barque,
Whose worth's unknown although his height be taken.
Love's not time's fool, though rosy lips and cheeks
Within his bending sickle's compass come;
Love alters not with his brief hours and weeks,
But bears it out even to the edge of doom.
    If this be error and upon me proved,
    I never writ, nor no man ever loved.

Sonnet 116

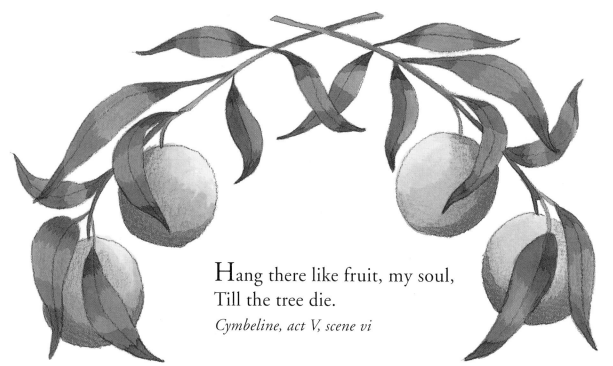

Hang there like fruit, my soul,
Till the tree die.

Cymbeline, act V, scene vi

THE ENVIOUS COURT

Who loses and who wins, who's in, who's out.
King Lear, act V, scene iii

The art o'th' court,
As hard to leave as keep, whose top to climb
Is certain falling, or so slipp'ry that
The fear's as bad as falling.
Cymbeline, act III, scene iii

If God have lent a man any manners he may easily put it off at court. He that cannot make a leg, put off's cap, kiss his hand, and say nothing, has neither leg, hands, lip nor cap, and indeed such a fellow, to say precisely, were not for the court.

All's Well That Ends Well, act II, scene ii

A certain lord, neat and trimly dressed,
Fresh as a bridegroom, and his chin, new-reaped,
Showed like a stubble-land at harvest-home.
He was perfumèd like a milliner,
And 'twixt his finger and his thumb he held
A pouncet-box, which ever and anon
He gave his nose and took't away again.

Henry IV, Part I, act I, scene iii

Those that are good manners at the court are as ridiculous in the country as the behaviour of the country is most mockable at the court. You told me you salute not at the court but you kiss your hands. That courtesy would be uncleanly if courtiers were shepherds. . . The courtier's hands are perfumed with civet.

As You Like It, act III, scene ii

This fellow pecks up wit as pigeons peas,
And utters it again when God doth please.
He is wit's pedlar, and retails his wares
At wakes and wassails, meetings, markets, fairs...
This gallant pins the wenches on his sleeve.
Had he been Adam, he had tempted Eve...
This is the ape of form, Monsieur Le Nice,
That when he plays at tables chides the dice
In honourable terms. Nay, he can sing
A mean most meanly, and in ushering
Mend him who can. The ladies call him sweet.
The stairs as he treads on them kiss his feet.
Love's Labour's Lost, act V, scene ii

Taffeta phrases, silken terms precise,
Three-piled hyperboles, spruce affectation,
Figures pedantical...
Love's Labour's Lost, act V, scene ii

These fellows of infinite tongue, that can rhyme themselves
into ladies' favours, they do always reason themselves out again.
Henry V, act V, scene ii

A courtier... could say, "Good morrow, sweet lord. How dost thou, good lord?" This might be my lord such a one, that praised my lord such a one's horse when a meant to beg it.

Hamlet, act V, scene i

Not a courtier—
Although they wear their faces to the bent
Of the King's looks—hath a heart that is not
Glad of the thing they scowl at.

Cymbeline, act I, scene i

There's no art
To find the mind's construction in the face.

Macbeth, act I, scene iv

When I tell him he hates flatterers;
He says he does, being then most flattered.

Julius Caesar, act II, scene i

THE KING IS BUT A MAN

Some are born great, some achieve greatness, and some have greatness thrust upon 'em.

Twelfth Night, act II, scene v

Not all the water in the rough rude sea
Can wash the balm from an anointed king.
The breath of worldly men cannot depose
The deputy elected by the Lord.

Richard II, act III, scene ii

I think the King is but a man, as I am.
The violet smells to him as it doth to me;
the element shows to him as it doth to me.
All his senses have but human conditions.
His ceremonies laid by, in his nakedness he
appears but a man, and though his affections
are higher mounted than ours, yet when they
stoop, they stoop with the like wing.

Henry V, act IV, scene i

How many thousand of my poorest subjects
Are at this hour asleep? O sleep, O gentle sleep,
Nature's soft nurse, how have I frighted thee,
That thou no more wilt weigh my eyelids down
And steep my senses in forgetfulness?
Why rather, sleep, liest thou in smoky cribs,
Upon uneasy pallets stretching thee,
And hushed with buzzing night-flies to thy slumber,
Than in the perfumed chambers of the great,
Under the canopies of costly state,
And lulled with sound of sweetest melody?
O thou dull god, why li'st thou with the vile
In loathsome beds, and leav'st the kingly couch
A watch-case, or a common 'larum-bell?
Wilt thou upon the high and giddy mast
Seal up the ship-boy's eyes, and rock his brains
In cradle of the rude imperious surge,
And in the visitation of the winds,
Who take the ruffian billows by the top,
Curling their monstrous heads, and hanging them
With deafing clamour in the slippery clouds,
That, with the hurly, death itself awakes?
Canst thou, O partial sleep, give thy repose
To the wet sea-boy in an hour so rude,
And in the calmest and most stillest night,
With all appliances and means to boot,
Deny it to a king? Then happy low, lie down.
Uneasy lies the head that wears a crown.
Henry IV, Part II, act III, scene i

I swear, 'tis better to be lowly born
And range with humble livers in content
Than to be perked up in a glist'ring grief
And wear a golden sorrow.

Henry VIII, act II, scene iii

Ah, what a life were this! How sweet! How lovely!
Gives not the hawthorn bush a sweeter shade
To shepherds looking on their seely sheep
Than doth a rich embroidered canopy
To kings that fear their subjects' treachery?

Henry VI, Part III, act II, scene v

To be, or not to be; that is the question:
Whether 'tis nobler in the mind to suffer
The slings and arrows of outrageous fortune,
Or to take arms against a sea of troubles,
And, by opposing, end them. To die, to sleep—
No more, and by a sleep to say we end
The heartache and the thousand natural shocks
That flesh is heir to—'tis a consummation
Devoutly to be wished. To die, to sleep.
To sleep, perchance to dream. Ay, there's the rub,
For in that sleep of death what dreams may come
When we have shuffled off this mortal coil
Must give us pause. There's the respect
That makes calamity of so long life,
For who would bear the whips and scorns of time,
Th'oppressor's wrong, the proud man's contumely,
The pangs of disprized love, the law's delay,
The insolence of office, and the spurns
That patient merit of th'unworthy takes,
When he himself might his quietus make
With a bare bodkin? Who would these fardels bear,
To grunt and sweat under a weary life,
But that the dread of something after death,
The undiscovered country from whose bourn
No traveller returns, puzzles the will,
And makes us rather bear those ills we have
Than fly to others that we know not of?
Thus conscience does make cowards of us all.

Hamlet, act III, scene i

O God, I could be bounded in a nutshell and count myself a king of infinite space, were it not that I have bad dreams.

Hamlet, act II, scene ii

O I have passed a miserable night,
So full of fearful dreams, of ugly sights,
That as I am a Christian faithful man,
I would not spend another such a night
Though 'twere to buy a world of happy days,
So full of dismal terror was the time.

Richard III, act I, scene iv

O Lord! Methought what pain it was to drown,
What dreadful noise of waters in my ears,
What sights of ugly death within my eyes.
Methoughts I saw a thousand fearful wrecks,
Ten thousand men that fishes gnawed upon,
Wedges of gold, great ouches, heaps of pearl,
Inestimable stones, unvalued jewels,
All scattered in the bottom of the sea.
Some lay in dead men's skulls; and in those holes
Where eyes did once inhabit, there were crept—
As 'twere in scorn of eyes—reflecting gems,
Which wooed the slimy bottom of the deep
And mocked the dead bones that lay scattered by.

Richard III, act I, scene iv

There is nothing either good or bad but thinking makes it so.
Hamlet, act II, scene ii

O that this too too solid flesh would melt,
Thaw, and resolve itself into a dew,
Or that the Everlasting had not fixed
His canon 'gainst self-slaughter! O God, O God,
How weary, stale, flat, and unprofitable
Seem to me all the uses of this world!
Fie on't, ah fie, fie! 'Tis an unweeded garden,
That grows to seed; things rank and gross in nature
Possess it merely.
Hamlet, act I, scene ii

Better be with the dead,
Whom we to gain our peace have sent to peace,
Than on the torture of the mind to lie
In restless ecstasy.
Macbeth, act III, scene ii

And I—like one lost in a thorny wood,
That rends the thorns and is rent with the thorns,
Seeking a way and straying from the way,
Not knowing how to find the open air,
But toiling desperately to find it out—
Torment myself to catch the English crown.
And from that torment I will free myself,
Or hew my way out with a bloody axe.
Henry VI, Part III, act III, scene ii

FIERCE CIVIL STRIFE

In cities, mutinies; in countries, discord; in palaces,
treason; and the bond cracked 'twixt son and father...
We have seen the best of our time. Machinations,
hollowness, treachery, and all ruinous disorders
follow us disquietly to our graves.

King Lear, act I, scene ii

And Liberty plucks Justice by the nose,
The baby beats the nurse, and quite athwart
Goes all decorum.

Measure for Measure, act I, scene iii

The children yet unborn
Shall feel this day as sharp to them as thorn.

Richard II, act IV, scene i

England now is left
To tug and scramble, and to part by th' teeth
The unowed interest of proud swelling state.
Now for the bare-picked bone of majesty
Doth doggèd war bristle his angry crest,
And snarleth in the gentle eyes of peace;
Now powers from home and discontents at home
Meet in one line, and vast confusion waits,
As doth a raven on a sick-fall'n beast,
The imminent decay of wrested pomp.
Now happy he whose cloak and cincture can
Hold out this tempest.

King John, act IV, scene iii

Blood and destruction shall be so in use,
And dreadful objects so familiar,
That mothers shall but smile when they behold
Their infants quartered with the hands of war.

Julius Caesar, act III, scene i

That England that was wont to conquer others
Hath made a shameful conquest of itself.

Richard II, act II, scene i

What must the King do now? Must he submit?
The King shall do it. Must he be deposed?
The King shall be contented. Must he lose
The name of King? A God's name, let it go.
I'll give my jewels for a set of beads,
My gorgeous palace for a hermitage,
My gay apparel for an almsman's gown,
My figured goblets for a dish of wood,
My sceptre for a palmer's walking staff,
My subjects for a pair of carvèd saints,
And my large kingdom for a little grave,
A little, little grave, an obscure grave;
Or I'll be buried in the King's highway,
Some way of common trade, where subjects' feet
May hourly trample on their sovereign's head,
For on my heart they tread now, whilst I live.

Richard II, act III, scene iii

O, now for ever
Farewell the tranquil mind, farewell content,
Farewell the plumèd troops, and the big wars
That makes ambition virtue! O, farewell,
Farewell the neighing steed and the shrill trump,
The spirit-stirring drum, th'ear-piercing fife,
The royal banner, and all quality,
Pride, pomp, and circumstance of glorious war!
And O, you mortal engines whose rude throats
Th'immortal Jove's dread clamours counterfeit,
Farewell! Othello's occupation's gone!

Othello, act III, scene iii

Reputation, reputation, reputation—O, I ha' lost my reputation,
I ha' lost the immortal part of myself, and what remains is bestial!

Othello, act II, scene iii

I have lived long enough. My way of life
Is fall'n into the sere, the yellow leaf,
And that which should accompany old age,
As honour, love, obedience, troops of friends,
I must not look to have, but in their stead,
Curses, not loud but deep, mouth-honour, breath
Which the poor heart would fain deny and dare not.

Macbeth, act V, scene iii

O let not virtue seek
Remuneration for the thing it was;
For beauty, wit,
High birth, vigour of bone, desert in service,
Love, friendship, charity, are subjects all
To envious and calumniating time.

Troilus and Cressida, act III, scene iii

Here I stand your slave,
A poor, infirm, weak and despised old man.

King Lear, act III, scene ii

Thus are my blossoms blasted in the bud,
And caterpillars eat my leaves away.

Henry VI, Part II, act III, scene i

I have touched the highest point of all my greatness,
And from that full meridian of my glory
I haste now to my setting. I shall fall
Like a bright exhalation in the evening,
And no man see me more.

Henry VIII, act III, scene ii

Life's but a walking shadow, a poor player
That struts and frets his hour upon the stage,
And then is heard no more. It is a tale
Told by an idiot, full of sound and fury,
Signifying nothing.

Macbeth, act V, scene v

O mighty Caesar! Dost thou lie so low?
Are all thy conquests, glories, triumphs, spoils,
Shrunk to this little measure?

Julius Caesar, act III, scene i

But a clod
And module of confounded royalty.

King John, act V, scene vii

OUR LIFE IS OF A MINGLED YARN

They say best men are moulded out of faults,
And, for the most, become much more the better
For being a little bad.

Measure for Measure, act V, scene i

Virtue that transgresses is but patched with sin,
and sin that amends is but patched with virtue.

Twelfth Night, act I, scene v

Roses have thorns, and silver fountains mud.
Clouds and eclipses stain both moon and sun.

Sonnet 35

What a piece of work is a man! How noble in reason, how infinite in faculty, in form and moving how express and admirable, in action how like an angel, in apprehension how like a god— the beauty of the world, the paragon of animals! And yet to me what is this quintessence of dust?

Hamlet, act II, scene ii

'Tis in ourselves that we are thus or thus. Our bodies are our gardens, to the which our wills are gardeners; so that if we will plant nettles or sow lettuce, set hyssop and weed up thyme, supply it with one gender of herbs or distract it with many, either to have it sterile with idleness or manured with industry, why, the power and corrigible authority of this lies in our wills.

Othello, act I, scene iii

Why should the worm intrude the maiden bud,
Or hateful cuckoos hatch in sparrows' nests,
Or toads infect fair founts with venom mud,
Or tyrant folly lurk in gentle breasts,
Or kings be breakers of their own behests?
   But no perfection is so absolute
   That some impurity doth not pollute.

The Rape of Lucrece, lines 848–854

If our virtues
Did not go forth of us, 'twere all alike
As if we had them not.

Measure for Measure, act I, scene i

My bounty is as boundless as the sea,
My love as deep. The more I give to thee
The more I have, for both are infinite.

Romeo and Juliet, act II, scene i

A friend should bear his friend's infirmities.

Julius Caesar, act IV, scene ii

Poor naked wretches, wheresoe'er you are,
That bide the pelting of this pitiless storm,
How shall your houseless heads and unfed sides,
Your looped and windowed raggedness, defend you
From seasons such as these? O, I have ta'en
Too little care of this. Take physic, pomp,
Expose thyself to feel what wretches feel,
That thou mayst shake the superflux to them
And show the heavens more just.

King Lear, act III, scene iv

Good name in man and woman, dear my lord,
Is the immediate jewel of their souls.
Who steals my purse steals trash; 'tis something, nothing;
'Twas mine, 'tis his, and has been slave to thousands.
But he that filches from me my good name
Robs me of that which not enriches him
And makes me poor indeed.

Othello, act III, scene iii

Rightly to be great
Is not to stir without great argument,
But greatly to find quarrel in a straw
When honour's at the stake.

Hamlet, act IV,
  scene iv

We few, we happy few, we band of brothers.
For he today that sheds his blood with me
Shall be my brother; be he ne'er so vile,
This day shall gentle his condition.
And gentlemen in England now abed
Shall think themselves accursed they were not here,
And hold their manhoods cheap whiles any speaks
That fought with us upon St Crispin's day.

Henry V, act IV, scene iii

I love
The name of honour more than I fear death.

Julius Caesar, act I, scene ii

Once more unto the breach, dear friends, once more,
Or close the wall up with our English dead.
In peace there's nothing so becomes a man
As modest stillness and humility,
But when the blast of war blows in our ears,
Then imitate the action of the tiger.
Stiffen the sinews, conjure up the blood,
Disguise fair nature with hard-favoured rage.
Then lend the eye a terrible aspect,
Let it pry through the portage of the head
Like the brass cannon, let the brow o'erwhelm it
As fearfully as doth a gallèd rock
O'erhang and jutty his confounded base,
Swilled with the wild and wasteful ocean.
Now set the teeth and stretch the nostril wide,
Hold hard the breath, and bend up every spirit
To his full height. On, on, you noblest English,
Whose blood is fet from fathers of war-proof,
Fathers that like so many Alexanders
Have in these parts from morn till even fought,
And sheathed their swords for lack of argument.
Dishonour not your mothers; now attest
That those whom you called fathers did
    beget you.

Henry V, act III, scene i

True nobility is exempt from fear.

Henry VI, Part II, act IV, scene i

There is a tide in the affairs of men
Which, taken at the flood, leads on to fortune;
Omitted, all the voyage of their life
Is bound in shallows and in miseries.
On such a full sea are we now afloat,
And we must take the current when it serves,
Or lose our ventures.

Julius Caesar, act IV, scene ii

Perseverance, dear my lord,
Keeps honour bright. To have done is to hang
Quite out of fashion, like a rusty mail
In monumental mock'ry.

Troilus and Cressida, act III, scene iii

How poor are they that ha' not patience!
What wound did ever heal but by degrees?

Othello, act II, scene iii

Give me that man
That is not passion's slave, and I will wear him
In my heart's core, ay, in my heart of heart,
As I do thee.

Hamlet, act III, scene ii

The better part of valour is discretion.
Henry IV, Part I, act V, scene iv

He that can endure
To follow with allegiance a fall'n lord
Does conquer him that did his master
    conquer.
Antony and Cleopatra, act III, scene xiii

This Duncan
Hath borne his faculties so meek, hath been
So clear in his great office, that his virtues
Will plead like angels, trumpet-tongued against
The deep damnation of his taking-off.
Macbeth, act I, scene vii

I will a round unvarnished tale deliver.
Othello, act I, scene iii

There are no tricks in plain and simple faith.
Julius Caesar, act IV, scene ii

Simple truth miscalled simplicity.
Sonnet 66

O, then we bring forth weeds
When our quick winds lie still.
Antony and Cleopatra, act I, scene ii

O, beware, my lord, of jealousy.
It is the green-eyed monster which doth mock
The meat it feeds on.
Othello, act III, scene iii

Rumour is a pipe
Blown by surmises, Jealousy's conjectures...
Henry IV, Part II, Induction

But 'tis a common proof
That lowliness is young ambition's ladder,
Whereto the climber-upward turns his face;
But when he once attains the upmost round,
He then unto the ladder turns his back,
Looks in the clouds, scorning the base degrees
By which he did ascend.
Julius Caesar, act II, scene i

Yon Cassius has a lean and hungry look.
He thinks too much. Such men are dangerous.
Julius Caesar, act I, scene ii

Cromwell, I charge thee, fling away ambition.
By that sin fell the angels.
Henry VIII, act III, scene ii

Everything includes itself in power,
Power into will, will into appetite;
And appetite, an universal wolf...
Must make perforce an universal prey,
And last eat up himself.
Troilus and Cressida, act I, scene iii

Through tattered clothes great vices do appear;
Robes and furred gowns hide all. Plate sin with gold,
And the strong lance of justice hurtless breaks;
Arm it in rags, a pigmy's straw does pierce it.
King Lear, act IV, scene v

See how yon justice rails upon yon simple thief...
change places, and handy-dandy, which is the justice,
which is the thief.
King Lear, act IV, scene vi

O, it is excellent
To have a giant's strength, but it is tyrannous
To use it like a giant.
Measure for Measure, act II, scene ii

They are as sick that surfeit with too much
as they that starve with nothing.
Merchant of Venice, act I, scene ii

Like an eagle in a dove-cote...
Coriolanus, act V, scene vi

Is this a dagger which I see before me,
The handle toward my hand?

Macbeth, act II, scene i

Between the acting of a dreadful thing
And the first motion, all the interim is
Like a phantasma or a hideous dream.
The genius and the mortal instruments
Are then in counsel, and the state of man,
Like to a little kingdom, suffers then
The nature of an insurrection.

Julius Caesar, act II, scene i

The colour of the King doth come and go
Between his purpose and his conscience,
Like heralds 'twixt two dreadful battles set.
His passion is so ripe it needs must break.

King John, act IV, scene ii

To hell, allegiance! Vows to the blackest devil!
Conscience and grace to the profoundest pit!
I dare damnation.

Hamlet, act IV, scene v

Why, I can smile, and murder whiles I smile,
And cry "Content!" to that which grieves my heart,
And wet my cheeks with artificial tears,
And frame my face to all occasions.

Henry VI, Part III, act III, scene ii

Unsex me here,
And fill me from the crown to the toe top-full
Of direst cruelty.

Macbeth, act I, scene v

Savage, extreme, rude, cruel, not to trust.

Sonnet 129

I am one, my liege,
Whom the vile blows and buffets of the world
Hath so incensed that I am reckless what
I do to spite the world.

Macbeth, act III, scene i

But man, proud man,
Dressed in a little brief authority…
…like an angry ape
Plays such fantastic tricks before high heaven
As makes the angels weep.

Measure for Measure, act II, scene ii

Get thee glass eyes,
And, like a scurvy politician, seem
To see the things thou dost not.

King Lear, act IV, scene v

Look like the innocent flower,
But be the serpent under't.

Macbeth, act I, scene v

A goodly apple rotten at the heart.
O, what a goodly outside falsehood hath!

The Merchant of Venice, act I, scene iii

…Oaths are straws, men's faiths are
wafer-cakes,
And Holdfast is the only dog, my duck.

Henry V, act II, scene iii

The devil can cite Scripture for his purpose.

The Merchant of Venice, act I, scene iii

...Breaking his oath and resolution like
A twist of rotten silk.

Coriolanus, act V, scene vi

The hearts
That spanieled me at heels, to whom I gave
Their wishes, do discandy, melt their sweets
On blossoming Caesar; and this pine is barked,
That overtopped them all.

Antony and Cleopatra, act IV, scene xiii

Oftentimes to win us to our harm
The instruments of darkness tell us truths,
Win us with honest trifles to betray's
In deepest consequence.

Macbeth, act I, scene iii

Has friendship such a faint and milky heart
It turns in less than two nights?

Timon of Athens, act III, scene i

Friendship is constant in all other things
Save in the office and affairs of love.
Therefore all hearts in love use their own tongues.
Let every eye negotiate for itself,
And trust no agent; for beauty is a witch
Against whose charms faith melteth into blood.

Much Ado About Nothing, act II, scene i

Look as I blow this feather from my face,
And as the air blows it to me again,
Obeying with my wind when I do blow,
And yielding to another when it blows,
Commanded always by the greater gust—
Such is the lightness of you common men.

Henry VI, Part III, act III, scene i

Our slippery people,
Whose love is never linked to the deserver
Till his deserts are passed.

Antony and Cleopatra, act I, scene ii

It hath been taught us from the primal state
That he which is was wished until he were,
And the ebbed man, ne'er loved till ne'er worth love,
Comes deared by being lacked. This common body,
Like to a vagabond flag upon the stream,
Goes to, and back, lackeying the varying tide,
To rot itself with motion.

Antony and Cleopatra, act I, scene iv

They'll take suggestion as a cat laps milk.

The Tempest, act II, scene i

I hate ingratitude more in a man
Than lying, vainness, babbling drunkenness,
Or any taint of vice whose strong corruption
Inhabits our frail blood.

Twelfth Night, act III, scene iv

Blow, winds, and crack your cheeks! Rage, blow,
You cataracts and hurricanoes, spout
Till you have drenched our steeples, drowned the cocks!
You sulph'rous and thought-executing fires,
Vaunt-couriers of oak-cleaving thunderbolts,
Singe my white head; and thou all-shaking thunder,
Strike flat the thick rotundity o'th' world,
Crack nature's moulds, all germens spill at once
That makes ingrateful man.

King Lear, act III, scene ii

How sharper than a serpent's tooth it is
To have a thankless child.

King Lear, act I, scene iv

All the stored vengeances of heaven fall
On her ingrateful top! Strike her young bones,
You taking airs, with lameness! . . .
You nimble lightnings, dart your blinding flames
Into her scornful eyes. Infect her beauty,
You fen-sucked fogs drawn by the pow'rful sun
To fall and blister.

King Lear, act II, scene ii

Now does he feel
His secret murders sticking on his hands.
Macbeth, act V, scene ii

Will all great Neptune's ocean wash this blood
Clean from my hand? No, this my hand will rather
The multitudinous seas incarnadine,
Making the green one red.
Macbeth, act II, scene ii

Here's the smell of the blood still. All the perfumes
of Arabia will not sweeten this little hand. O, O, O!
Macbeth, act V, scene i

And thus the whirligig of time brings in his revenges.
Twelfth Night, act V, scene i

Bow, stubborn knees; and heart with strings of steel,
Be soft as sinews of the new-born babe.
All may be well.

Hamlet, act III, scene iii

O sovereign mistress of true melancholy...
                    Throw my heart
Against the flint and hardness of my fault.

Antony and Cleopatra, act IV, scene x

The rarer action is
In virtue than in vengeance. They being penitent,
The sole drift of my purpose doth extend
Not a frown further. Go release them, Ariel.

The Tempest, act V, scene i

The quality of mercy is not strained.
It droppeth as the gentle rain from heaven
Upon the place beneath. It is twice blest:
It blesseth him that gives, and him that takes.

The Merchant of Venice, act IV, scene i

No ceremony that to great ones 'longs,
Not the king's crown, nor the deputed sword,
The marshal's truncheon, nor the judge's robe,
Become them with one half so good a grace
As mercy does.

Measure for Measure, act II, scene ii

This is the excellent foppery of the world: that when we are sick in fortune—
often the surfeits of our own behaviour—we make guilty of our disasters the sun,
the moon, and stars, as if we were villains on necessity, fools by heavenly
compulsion, knaves, thieves, and treachers by spherical predominance,
drunkards, liars, and adulterers by an enforced obedience of planetary influence,
and all that we are evil in by a divine thrusting on.

King Lear, act I, scene ii

The fault, dear Brutus, is not in our stars,
But in ourselves, that we are underlings.

Julius Caesar, act I, scene ii

Use every man after his desert, and who
should 'scape whipping?

Hamlet, act II, scene ii

How would you be
If He which is the top of judgement should
But judge you as you are?

Measure for Measure, act II, scene ii

If there be
Yet left in heaven as small a drop of pity
As a wren's eye...

Cymbeline, act IV, scene ii

So our virtues
Lie in th'interpretation of the time.

Coriolanus, act IV, scene vii

Pray you now, forget
And forgive.

King Lear, act IV, scene vi

A peace above all earthly dignities,
A still and quiet conscience.

Henry VIII, act III, scene ii

So shines a good deed in a naughty world.

The Merchant of Venice, act V, scene i

OUR REVELS NOW ARE ENDED

Like as the waves make towards the pebbled shore,
So do our minutes hasten to their end,
Each changing place with that which goes before;
In sequent toil all forwards do contend.
Nativity, once in the main of light,
Crawls to maturity, wherewith being crowned
Crookèd eclipses 'gainst his glory fight,
And time that gave, doth now his gift confound.
Time doth transfix the flourish set on youth,
And delves the parallels in beauty's brow;
Feeds on the rarities of nature's truth,
And nothing stands but for his scythe to mow:
    And yet to times in hope my verse shall stand,
    Praising thy worth despite his cruel hand.

Sonnet 60

Let's do it after the high Roman fashion,
And make death proud to take us.
Antony and Cleopatra, act IV, scene xvi

If I must die,
I will encounter darkness as a bride,
And hug it in mine arms.
Measure for Measure, act III, scene i

Give me my Romeo, and when I shall die
Take him and cut him out in little stars,
And he will make the face of heaven so fine
That all the world will be in love with night
And pay no worship to the garish sun.
Romeo and Juliet, act III, scene ii

Death lies on her like an untimely frost
Upon the sweetest flower of all the field.
Romeo and Juliet, act IV, scene iv

Death, that hath sucked the honey of thy breath,
Hath had no power yet upon thy beauty.
Thou art not conquered. Beauty's ensign yet
Is crimson in thy lips and in thy cheeks,
And death's pale flag is not advancèd there.
Romeo and Juliet, act V, scene iii

Eyes, look your last.
Arms, take your last embrace, and lips, O you
The doors of breath, seal with a righteous kiss
A dateless bargain to engrossing death.
Romeo and Juliet, act V, scene iii

The bright day is done,
And we are for the dark.

*Antony and Cleopatra, act V,
scene ii*

O, withered is the garland of the war.
The soldier's pole is fall'n. Young boys and girls
Are level now with men. The odds is gone,
And there is nothing left remarkable
Beneath the visiting moon.

Antony and Cleopatra, act IV, scene xvi

Howl, howl, howl, howl! O, you are men of stones.
Had I your tongues and eyes, I'd use them so
That heaven's vault should crack. She's gone for ever.
I know when one is dead and when one lives.
She's dead as earth. Lend me a looking-glass.
If that her breath will mist or stain the stone,
Why, then she lives...
This feather stirs. She lives. If it be so,
It is a chance which does redeem all sorrows
That ever I have felt.

King Lear, act V, scene iii

My particular grief
Is of so floodgate and o'erbearing nature
That it engluts and swallows other sorrows,
And it is still itself.

Othello, act I, scene iii

Here is my journey's end, here is my butt
And very sea-mark of my utmost sail.

Othello, act V, scene ii

Fear no more the heat o'th' sun,
    Nor the furious winter's rages.
Thou thy worldly task hast done,
    Home art gone, and ta'en thy wages.
Golden lads and girls all must,
As chimney-sweepers, come to dust.

Fear no more the frown o'th' great,
    Thou art past the tyrant's stroke.
Care no more to clothe and eat,
    To thee the reed is as the oak.
The sceptre, learning, physic, must
All follow this, and come to dust.

Fear no more the lightning flash,
    Nor th'all-dreaded thunder-stone.
Fear not slander, censure rash.
    Thou hast finished joy and moan.
All lovers young, all lovers must
Consign to thee, and come to dust.
    No exorciser harm thee,
    Nor no witchcraft charm thee.
    Ghost unlaid forbear thee.
    Nothing ill come near thee.
    Quiet consummation have,
    And renownèd be thy grave!

Cymbeline, act IV, scene ii

Cowards die many times before their deaths;
The valiant never taste of death but once.
Of all the wonders that I yet have heard,
It seems to me most strange that men should fear,
Seeing that death, a necessary end,
Will come when it will come.

Julius Caesar, act II, scene ii

There's a divinity that shapes our ends,
Rough-hew them how we will.

Hamlet, act V, scene ii

Men must endure
Their going hence even as their coming hither.
Ripeness is all.

King Lear, act V, scene ii

Thou hast nor youth nor age,
But as it were an after-dinner's sleep
Dreaming on both.

Measure for Measure, act III, scene i

Full fathom five thy father lies.
  Of his bones are coral made;
Those are pearls that were his eyes;
  Nothing of him that doth fade
But doth suffer a sea-change
Into something rich and strange.
Sea-nymphs hourly ring his knell:
    Hark, now I hear them.
    Ding-dong bell.

The Tempest, act I, scene ii

God give them wisdom that have it; and those that are fools,
let them use their talents.

Twelfth Night, act I, scene v

FESTE
Good madonna, why mournest thou?

OLIVIA
Good fool, for my brother's death.

FESTE
I think his soul is in hell, madonna.

OLIVIA
I know his soul is in heaven, fool.

FESTE
The more fool, madonna, to mourn for
your brother's soul, being in heaven.

Twelfth Night, act I, scene v

I had rather have a fool to make me merry
than experience to make me sad.

As You Like It, act IV, scene i

The man that hath no music in himself,
Nor is not moved with concord of sweet sounds,
Is fit for treasons, stratagems, and spoils.
The Merchant of Venice, act V, scene i

In sweet music is such art,
Killing care and grief of heart.
Henry VIII, act III, scene i

The poet's eye, in a fine frenzy rolling,
Doth glance from heaven to earth, from earth to heaven,
And as imagination bodies forth
The forms of things unknown, the poet's pen
Turns them to shapes, and gives to airy nothing
A local habitation and a name.
A Midsummer Night's Dream, act V, scene i

Think, when we talk of horses, that you see them,
Printing their proud hoofs i'th' receiving earth;
For 'tis your thoughts that now must deck our kings,
Carry them here and there, jumping o'er times,
Turning th'accomplishment of many years
Into an hourglass.
Henry V, prologue to Act I

…To hold as 'twere the mirror up to nature.
Hamlet, act III, scene ii

All the world's a stage,
And all the men and women merely players.
They have their exits and their entrances,
And one man in his time plays many parts,
His acts being seven ages. At first the infant,
Mewling and puking in the nurse's arms.
Then the whining schoolboy, with his satchel,
And shining morning face, creeping like snail
Unwillingly to school. And then the lover,
Sighing like furnace, with a woeful ballad
Made to his mistress' eyebrow. Then, a soldier,
Full of strange oaths, and bearded like the pard,
Jealous in honour, sudden, and quick in quarrel,
Seeking the bubble reputation
Even in the cannon's mouth. And then the justice,
In fair round belly with good capon lined,
With eyes severe and beard of formal cut,
Full of wise saws and modern instances;
And so he plays his part. The sixth age shifts
Into the lean and slippered pantaloon,
With spectacles on nose and pouch on side,
His youthful hose, well saved, a world too wide
For his shrunk shank, and his big, manly voice,
Turning again toward childish treble, pipes
And whistles in his sound. Last scene of all,
That ends this strange, eventful history,
Is second childishness and mere oblivion,
Sans teeth, sans eyes, sans taste, sans everything.

As You Like It, act II, scene vii

Our revels now are ended. These our actors,
As I foretold you, were all spirits, and
Are melted into air, into thin air:
And like the baseless fabric of this vision,
The cloud-capped towers, the gorgeous palaces,
The solemn temples, the great globe itself,
Yea, all which it inherit, shall dissolve;
And, like this insubstantial pageant faded,
Leave not a rack behind. We are such stuff
As dreams are made on, and our little life
Is rounded with a sleep.

The Tempest, act IV, scene i

A great while ago the world begun,
    With hey ho, the wind and the rain,
But that's all one, our play is done,
    And we'll strive to please you every day.

Twelfth Night, act V, scene i

William Shakespeare

William Shakespeare was the son of John Shakespeare, a glove maker and wool dealer, and Mary Arden, the daughter of a well-to-do farmer. He was born in Stratford-upon-Avon in Warwickshire and baptized there on April 26, 1564. He married Anne Hathaway in 1582, and in the next few years they had three children.

Shakespeare moved to London in about 1587. For the next twenty-five years he lived and worked in London, though he always maintained his links with Stratford. Shakespeare worked as an actor and a playwright and was also busy in the management of the acting companies he belonged to. Eventually he became a permanent and leading member of a great acting company called The King's Men.

Shakespeare returned to live in Stratford in about 1610 and continued to write, at least until 1613. He died on April 23, 1616, aged fifty-two, and in 1623, a monument was erected to him in Holy Trinity Church. Shortly afterward, two of his friends and colleagues from the King's Men published his collected plays in an edition that became known as the First Folio.

✦ SHAKESPEARE'S PLAYS AND POETRY ✦

Numbers refer to pages on which the plays or poems have been quoted.

◆ *INDEX OF FIRST LINES* ◆

I know a bank where the wild thyme blows   12
I love the name of honour   62
I swear 'tis better to be lowly born   49
I think the King is but a man, as I am   47
I was too young that time to value her   26
I will a round unvarnished tale deliver   65
I will tell you   34
If God have lent a man any manners   44
If I must die   80
If music be the food of love, play on   37
If our virtues   61
If there be   77
If thou rememberest not the slightest folly   31
In cities, mutinies; in countries, discord   53
In love—ay, faith, to the very tip of the nose   33
In sweet music is such art   87
In the most high and palmy state of Rome   16
Is all the counsel that we two have shared   26
Is this a dagger which I see before me   68
It hath been taught us from the primal state   72
It was a lover and his lass   29

Kissing with golden face the meadows green   22

Let me not to the marriage of true minds   42
Let's do it after the high Roman fashion   80
Life's but a walking shadow, a poor player   58
Light thickens, and the crow   15
Like an eagle in a dove-cote   67
Like as the waves make towards the pebbled shore   79
Lo, here the gentle lark, weary of rest   21
Look as I blow this feather from my face   72
Look like the innocent flower   70
Love's feeling is more soft and sensible   39

Men must endure   85
Merrily, merrily shall I live now   11
Music, moody food of us that trade in love   37
My bounty is as boundless as the sea   61
My particular grief   83
My salad days   27

Night's candles are burnt out, and jocund day   22
No ceremony that to great ones 'longs   76

Not a courtier   46
Not all the water in the rough rude sea   47
Now does he feel   75
Now o'er the one half-world   17

O, beware, my lord, of jealousy   66
O Corin, that thou knew'st how I do love her   28
O coz, coz, coz, my pretty little coz   32
O God, I could be bounded in a nutshell   51
O happy fair   33
O I have passed a miserable night   51
O, it is excellent   67
O let not virtue seek   57
O Lord! Methought what pain it was to drown   51
O mighty Caesar! Dost thou lie so low   58
O, now for ever   56
O, she doth teach the torches to burn bright   33
O sovereign mistress of true melancholy   76
O that this too too solid flesh would melt   52
O, then we bring forth weeds   66
O, withered is the garland of the war   82
Oaths are straws, men's faiths are wafer-cakes   70
Oftentimes to win us to our harm   71
Once more unto the breach, dear friends, once more   63
Or as the snail, whose tender horns being hit   39
Our revels now are ended. These our actors   90
Our slippery people   72
Over hill, over dale   12

Peaseblossom, Cobweb, Mote, and Mustardseed   14
Perseverance, dear my lord   64
Poor naked wretches, wheresoe'er you are   61
Pray you now, forget   78
Proceed, sweet Cupid, thou hast thumped him   31

Reputation, reputation, reputation   56
Rightly to be great   62
Roses have thorns, and silver fountains mud   59
Round about the cauldron go   19
Rumour is a pipe   66

Savage, extreme, rude, cruel, not to trust   69
See how yon justice rails upon yon simple thief   67
She bids you on the wanton rushes lay you down   13

Simple truth miscalled simplicity   65
So holy and so perfect is my love   41
So our virtues   78
So shines a good deed in a naughty world   78
Some are born great   47
Some say thy fault is youth, some wantonness   27

Taffeta phrases, silken terms precise   45
Tell me where is fancy bred   32
That England that was wont to conquer others   55
That I might sleep out this great gap of time   40
The art o'th' court   43
The better part of valour is discretion   65
The bright day is done   82
The children yet unborn   53
The colour of the King doth come and go   68
The course of true love never did run smooth   41
The devil can cite Scripture for his purpose   70
The fault, dear Brutus, is not in our stars   77
The hearts that spanieled me   71
The man that hath no music in himself   87
The moon shines bright.... In such a night   36
The night has been unruly. Where we lay   20
The poet's eye, in a fine frenzy rolling   87
The quality of mercy is not strained   76
The rarer action is   76
The time has been   16
The tongues of mocking wenches are as keen   27
There are no tricks in plain and simple faith   65
There is a tide in the affairs of men   64
There is nothing either good or bad   52
There's a divinity that shapes our ends   85
There's no art   46
These fellows of infinite tongue   45
They are as sick that surfeit with too much   67
They say best men are moulded out of faults   59
They'll take suggestion as a cat laps milk   72
Think not I love him, though I ask for him   27
Think, when we talk of horses, that you see them   87
This Duncan   65
This fellow pecks up wit as pigeons peas   45
This is the excellent foppery of the world   77
Those that are good manners at the court   44
Thou art thy mother's glass, and she in thee   24

Thou hast nor youth nor age   85
Through tattered clothes great vices do appear   67
Through the house give glimmering light   14
Thus are my blossoms blasted in the bud   57
'Tis in ourselves that we are thus or thus   60
'Tis now the very witching time of night   16
To be, or not to be; that is the question   50
To hell, allegiance! Vows to the blackest devil   69
To hold as 'twere the mirror up to nature   87
True nobility is exempt from fear   63

Under the greenwood tree   10
Unsex me here   69
Use every man after his desert   77

Virtue that transgresses is but patched with sin   59

We few, we happy few, we band of brothers   62
We were as twinned lambs that did frisk i'th' sun   25
We were, fair Queen   25
What a piece of work is a man   60
What are these   17
What is love? 'Tis not hereafter   28
What must the King do now? Must he submit   55
What stature is she of   33
When I tell him he hates flatterers   46
When shall we three meet again   18
When you speak, sweet   37
Where the bee sucks, there suck I   12
Who loses and who wins, who's in, who's out   43
Why, how know you that I am in love   30
Why, I can smile, and murder whiles I smile   69
Why should the worm intrude the maiden bud   60
Will all great Neptune's ocean wash this blood   75

Yon Cassius has a lean and hungry look   66
You spotted snakes with double tongue   13

✦ SELECT GLOSSARY ✦

Aeson, king of Iolcos. His youth was restored by Medea.

alchemy, a transforming power

Alexanders, refers to Alexander the Great, King of Macedonia, conqueror of Egypt and the eastern half of the Greek empire

axle-tree, axle

barked, stripped of bark

barque, boat, ship

behests, commands

birdbolt, blunt-headed arrow for shooting birds

blast, a gust of wind

bodkin, dagger

bourn, a boundary

brazen, made of brass

butt, end

cabinet, dwelling

calumniating, slanderous

canstick, candlestick

cherubin, cherub

cincture, belt

cloy, become distasteful from excess

conceits, ideas

confounded, damned, blasted

consummation, perfection

corrigible, able to be corrected

couriers, messengers

coz'ning, cheating

Cressid, Cressida, daughter of Calchas, a Trojan priest. She was beloved by Troilus, a Trojan prince.

Cupid, god of love, son of Venus and Mars

damask, material woven with a pattern

deared, valued

dewberries, blackberries

Dido, Queen of Carthage, who fell in love with Aeneas. When he deserted her she committed suicide by throwing herself upon a pyre.

discandy, dissolve

eglantine, wild rose

fardels, burdens

fen-sucked, drawn out of bogs

fenny, from the fens

fet, derived

filches, steals

flag, iris or reed-grass

foppery, folly, deceit

gallèd, unpleasant, swollen

genius, spirit

germens, seeds

grandam, grandmother

Hecate, the chief or goddess of witches

hie, to hasten

hyperbole, extravagant exaggeration

hyssop, an aromatic plant

imposition, accusation

incarnadine, dye red

jocund, merry

Jove, poetic form of Jupiter, ruler of the gods

Juno, queen of the gods and wife of Jupiter

lackeying, slavishly following or attending

lays, songs

lodestar, the Pole Star, the star that guides

machinations, crafty scheme or plot

mail, defensive armor for the body

Medea, an enchantress

meridian, midday

module, model, image

Neptune, god of the sea

orbs, spheres

orthography, a person skilled in the art of spelling

ouches, jewels

pap, breast

paragon, model of excellence

pard, panther or leopard

phantasma, illusion

Philomel, the nightingale personified in Greek mythology

Phoebus, Apollo, god of the Sun

physic, medicine

portage, portholes

pouncet-box, small box for perfumes

quietus, release from life

quintessence, the most essential part of something

rack, trace

sans, without

Saturn, god of Agriculture

sea-mark, a mark of tidal limit

seely, harmless

sequent, succeeding, following

sere, withered

shank, the leg from knee to foot

superflux, surplus

tabor, small drum

tallow, fat used for making candles

Tarquin, son of the king of Rome in Shakespeare's *The Rape of Lucrece,* who is banished after raping Lucretia

Thisbe, lover of Pyramus. They agreed to meet at a tomb outside the city of Babylon but Thisbe was frightened by a lion and fled, dropping her cloak, which the lion tore apart. Pyramus found it, thought she had been killed by the lion, and committed suicide. When she found him, Thisbe killed herself on his sword.

thunder-stone, thunderbolt

Titania, queen of fairyland, wife of Oberon

Troilus, a prince of Troy, lover of Cressida

tun'd spheres, the concentric globes supposed to revolve around the earth with a harmonious sound

vaunt-couriers, heralds

Venus, goddess of love and beauty

vestal, chaste

wafer-cakes, very thin crisp cake

wanned, turned pale and sickly

wassails, feasts

weed, garment

whirligig, a merry-go-round

Friends, Romans, countrymen, lend me your ears ✦ Down on your knees and thank heaven, fasting, for

...st loving, mere foll... ...rs that never felt a wound ✦ Out

...ind ✦ Men have died from time to ...ten them, but not for love ✦ The Prin...

arbitrator Time will one day end it ✦ How beauteous mankind is! O brave new world that ha...

A snapper-up of unconsidered trifles ✦ O my prophetic soul! ✦ I have not slept on...

✦ Why was he sent into England? Why, because a was mad. A shall recover his wits there;

of nothing. Speak again ✦ We have scorched the snake, not killed it ✦ I can call spirits f...

them? ✦ Men's evil manners live in brass, their virtues we write in water ✦ I must be cr...

methinks ✦ Sweets to the sweet. Farewell ✦ He hath eaten me out of house and home ✦ More

than are dreamt of in our philosophy ✦ Never, never, never, never, never ✦ What's in a...

The time of life is short. To spend that shortness basely were too long ✦ A horse! A h...

better than figs ✦ He that dies pays all debts ✦ The very substance of the ambitiou...

ridiculous excess ✦ For love i... ...il...l th... for everything that he can com...

March ✦ O, my offence is... how apt the poor are to be proud! ...

conquest, for then both parti... ...es ✦ The play's the thing ✦ ...

had, all's spent, where our d... ...e of opinion! A man may wear it on...

Striving to better, oft we ma... ...y no means vulgar ✦ Men of fe...

pain ✦ What great ones a... ...hout all remedy should be without r...

good end ✦ It is a wise ...hild ✦ Beware of entrance to a...

sour ✦ Rich, not gaudy; ...e man ✦ More in sorrow than in...

are the uses of adversity ...ched but to fine issues ✦ Goo...

choice in rotten apples ✦ ...uch as mercy ✦ Oh, how bitter

eyes ✦ When sorrows come they come not single spies, but in battalions ✦ The worst is not so l...

proverbs ✦ Exit, pursued by a bear ✦ O Cupid, Cupid, Cupid! ✦ Letting "I dare not" wait upo...